Bella's
Best of All

Bella's Best of All

JAMIE HARPER

RP|KIDS

PHILADELPHIA • LONDON

Books published by Running Press are available at special discounts for bulk
purchases in the United States by corporations, institutions, and other organizations.
For more information, please contact the Special Markets Department at
the Perseus Books Group, 2300 Chestnut Street, Suite 200, Philadelphia, PA 19103,
or call (800) 810-4145, ext. 5000, or e-mail special.markets@perseusbooks.com.

ISBN 978-0-7624-5819-6
Library of Congress Control Number: 2015940930

9 8 7 6 5 4 3 2 1
Digit on the right indicates the number of this printing

Designed by Frances J. Soo Ping Chow
Edited by Marlo Scrimizzi
Typography: Brandon, Gonte, and Harman

The illustrations were done in block prints and mixed-media collage,
using watercolor, ink, and cut-paper.

Published by Running Press Kids
An Imprint of Running Press Book Publishers
A Member of the Perseus Books Group
2300 Chestnut Street
Philadelphia, PA 19103–4371

Visit us on the web!
www.runningpress.com/rpkids

For Blankie, Spidey, and Baba and all the loveys that are best of all.

My purse is good…

Mommy's is better.

My necklace is good…

Mommy's is better.

My shoes are good…

Mommy's are better.

My paint is good…

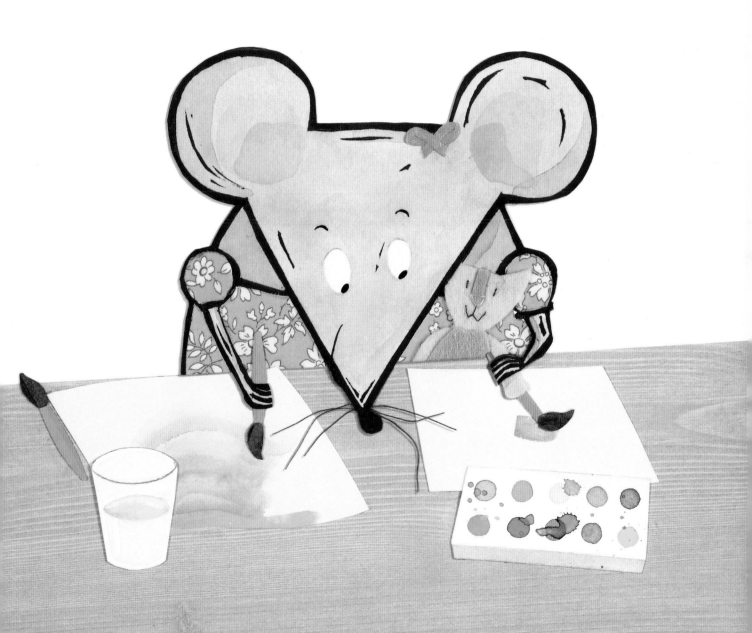

Mommy's is better.

My bubbles are good…

Mommy's are better.

My desk is good…

Mommy's is better.

My drum is good…

Mommy's are better.

My toys are good…

Mommy's are better.

My gown is good…

Mommy's is better.

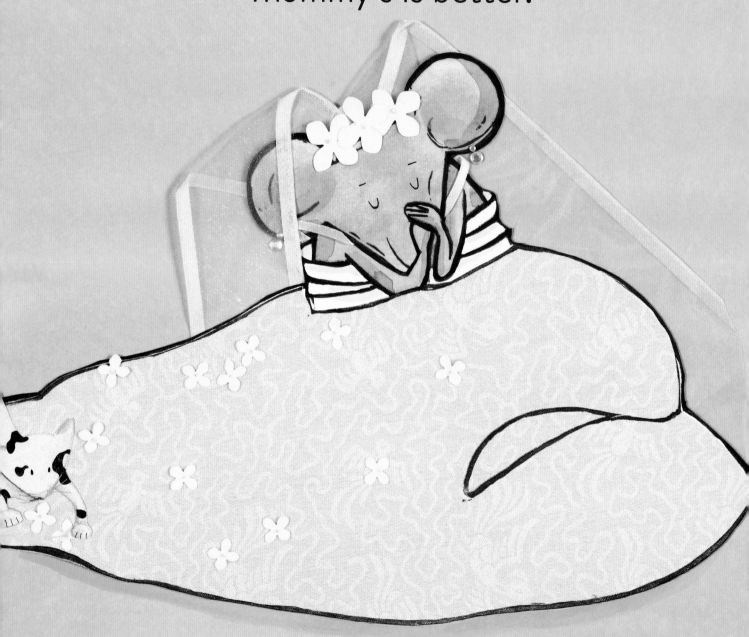

Mommy's cat is good...

My Kitty...

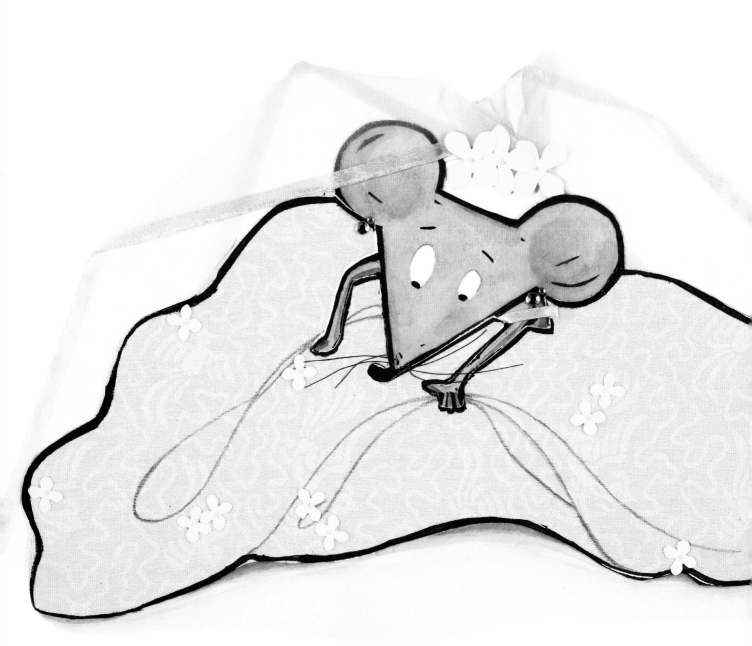

Kitty?

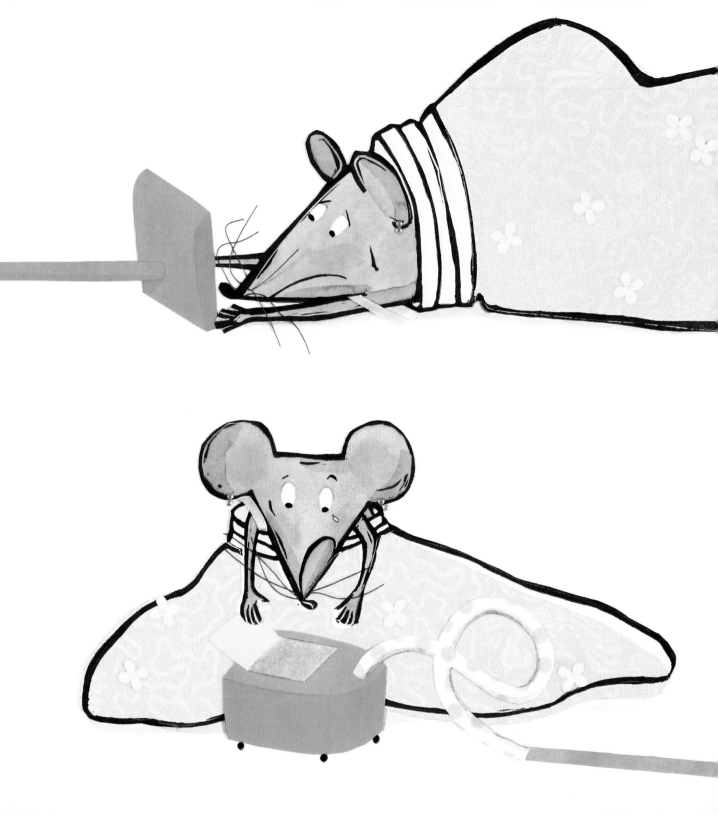

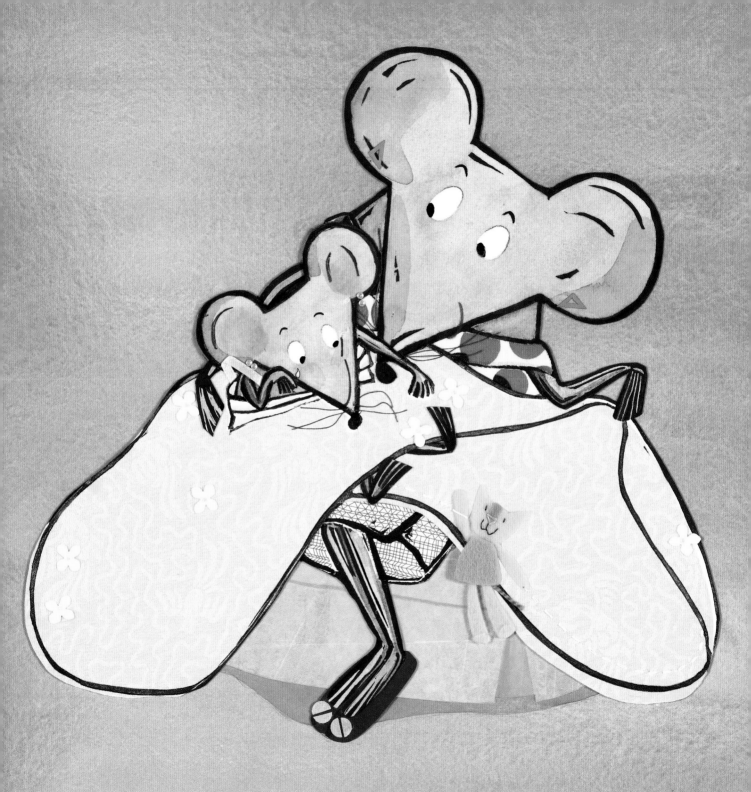

Mommy's stuff is good...

But Kitty is the best of all.